Brian's Brownies or Bobbseys' Cookies?

"Maybe you should work on a new cookie recipe," Brian told Freddie.

"There's nothing wrong with our recipe," Freddie replied.

"Yeah, we just can't find it," Flossie added.

Freddie cleared his throat. "What she means is that it's a *secret* recipe."

"I don't think anyone wants it," Brian scoffed. "Especially not after I start selling brownies *and* cookies."

"Why don't you give us back our recipe?" Flossie demanded. "We know you took it!"

"I didn't take your stupid recipe," said Brian. "I don't need it, anyway. You're just wasting your time!"

Books in The New Bobbsey Twins™ Series

Available from MINSTREL Books

BOBBSEY T?W·I·N·S

#22
The
Super-duper
Cookie
Caper

LAURA LEE HOPE
Illustrated by RANDY BERRETT

A MINSTREL® BOOK

PUBLISHED BY POCKET BOOKS

New York   London   Toronto   Sydney   Tokyo   Singapore

A MINSTREL PAPERBACK *ORIGINAL*

 A Minstrel Book published by
POCKET BOOKS, a division of Simon & Schuster
1230 Avenue of the Americas, New York, NY 10020

ISBN: 0-671-69294-1

First Minstrel Books printing February 1991

10 9 8 7 6 5 4 3 2 1

Contents

The
Super-duper
Cookie
Caper

1

A Sweet Idea

"Hey, Flossie, guess what?" Freddie Bobbsey asked his twin sister one Friday evening.

Flossie looked up from her book. "What?"

"I'm going to get a new bike," Freddie announced. He plunked himself down on Flossie's bed.

"How?" Flossie asked. She looked surprised.

"I have a great idea to make some money," Freddie said. "I guess you could help if you want. But it's going to take a lot of work."

"What do I have to do?" asked Flossie.

"Well, remember how many of Grandma's

cookies we sold at the school bake sale last week? Her special oatmeal chocolate chip cookies?"

Flossie nodded.

"I'm going to sell them on my own!" Freddie said.

Flossie giggled. "But you can't cook," she pointed out.

Freddie shrugged. "I'll learn. How hard can it be? I just can't do it all by myself."

Flossie shook her curly blond hair. "No way! I'm not helping you make cookies so you can get a dumb bike."

"I'd give you some of the money," Freddie promised.

Flossie folded her arms. "How much?"

"I'll have to figure that out," said Freddie. "But don't worry, it'll be a lot."

Flossie snapped her fingers. "I know! I can use the money for when I go to the big fair with Susie."

"You can have a quarter of everything I make," Freddie offered. "I mean, of everything *we* make."

"Well . . . okay," Flossie replied. "But I'm doing only a quarter of the work."

"All right," Freddie agreed. "I guess that's fair. Let's go downstairs and talk to Mom and Dad."

Mr. and Mrs. Bobbsey were in the living room, watching a movie with Nan and Bert. Nan and Bert were twins like Freddie and Flossie, but they had brown hair instead of blond. They were twelve years old. Freddie told them all about his plan.

"It sounds like a good idea," said Mrs. Bobbsey. "After all, everyone likes cookies."

"Where are you going to sell them?" asked Mr. Bobbsey. "In front of the house?"

"I don't know," said Freddie. "I haven't thought about that yet."

"Why don't you sell them at the park on weekends?" Nan suggested.

Freddie nodded eagerly. "Good idea."

"I don't know, Freddie. I can't see you as a chef," said Bert.

"Flossie's going to help," Freddie replied.

"You'll probably need more help than

that," said Mrs. Bobbsey, laughing. "I can give you a hand. I'll ask Mrs. Green if she can pitch in, too." Mrs. Green was the Bobbseys' housekeeper.

"So do you think we'll make any money?" Flossie asked.

"There's only one way to find out," said Mr. Bobbsey with a smile.

Freddie got up extra early the next morning. He wanted to make sure everything went right. He turned on his computer and called up his new program: Operation Bike. With Bert's help Freddie had figured out how much money he needed to make before summer vacation. He wanted to have his new bike by then.

Freddie stared at the screen. "If each cookie costs ten cents to make, and I sell it for thirty-five cents, then I'll earn twenty-five cents for every cookie," he muttered. Twenty-five cents didn't sound like much. But if he could sell a hundred cookies a day, he'd have the money in a few weeks!

Freddie switched off the computer and went

down to breakfast. "Ready to start baking?" his mother asked.

Freddie grinned. "I'm ready! Where's Flossie?" The rest of the family was sitting at the kitchen table.

"She's still in bed," said Nan.

Maybe asking Flossie to help had been a big mistake, Freddie thought. But his twin wandered into the kitchen a few minutes later, rubbing her eyes.

"Good morning!" Mr. Bobbsey said, greeting her. "Can I pour you some cereal, or would you like toast?"

"I think I'll just wait for the cookies," Flossie mumbled.

"You'll eat a good breakfast first," said Mrs. Bobbsey with a frown. "And we'd better get started, if you want to sell those cookies this afternoon."

She went into the pantry and got a small metal box. "Here's the recipe," she said. She handed a well-worn index card to Freddie. His grandmother had used a red pen to write down her special ingredients. The recipe looked about a hundred years old.

Freddie read the recipe. The first thing he needed was flour. He got a big bowl from the cupboard. Then he started to measure cups of flour into the bowl. "One, two," he counted out loud.

"Three, five, nine," Bert teased.

"Three," Freddie said a little louder. He wasn't going to let Bert mess him up. He was going to make enough money for his new bike, no matter what!

Around noon Freddie and Flossie took the cookies they had baked and went to the park. They sat at a picnic table near the front entrance. Flossie and Nan had made a big sign saying "Oatmeal Chocolate Chip Cookies— 35¢ each."

But after an hour went by, they had sold only a few.

"Maybe we're charging too much," said Flossie.

"Just wait until that baseball game ends," Freddie told her. "Then everyone will come over."

Sure enough, when the baseball game fin-

COOKI
OATMEA
CHOCOLAT
DOZ.

ished, a stream of kids headed right for their table.

"I'll take three," one of the older kids said. He tossed the money to Flossie.

"Thanks!" she said in surprise.

After that they sold about three dozen cookies in ten minutes.

"Great cookies!" one boy said.

"Will you be here every weekend?" asked another boy.

"Definitely," said Freddie.

"Excellent!" said the boy. "We'll be back." He and his friends headed off across the park.

A few minutes later Susie Larker, Flossie's best friend, came over.

"Hi!" she said. "How's it going?"

"Great!" said Flossie. "Want a cookie?"

"That's thirty-five cents," Freddie said.

"Freddie, she's my friend!" Flossie protested.

Freddie shook his head. "Sorry. No free samples."

Susie didn't look too happy, but she handed Freddie a quarter and a dime. Then she took a bite of the cookie. "This is delicious!" she said.

"We used Grandma Bobbsey's secret recipe," Flossie told her. "And Freddie is giving me part of the money we make."

"I bet you'll make a ton of money," said Susie.

"I can't wait for the fair," said Flossie. "We'll be able to go on every ride and play all the games."

"That'll be great," said Susie. "Can I have another cookie?"

After Susie left, some of the twins' classmates came by. Teddy Blake, Freddie's best friend, bought two cookies. Brian Mueller had four. Before they knew it, the twins were down to only five cookies!

At four o'clock they began packing up. As they were taking down their sign, a man walked over to them. The name Mike was stitched onto his shirt.

"Would you like some cookies?" Flossie asked.

The man peered at the remaining cookies. "Yeah, give me a couple." He gave Flossie a dollar, and Freddie held out the cookies. The dollar was covered with some kind of white powder. Flossie put the dollar in the money envelope. Then she brushed off her hands on her jeans and gave the man his change.

The man took a bite of cookie and chewed slowly, making a face.

"They're all right, but they're not great," he grumbled as he walked away.

"I wonder what's wrong with him," Flossie said.

"I guess he doesn't think much of Grandma's secret recipe," said Freddie. He put the top back on the almost empty cookie tin. "But it doesn't matter, because everyone else does," he said. "And I can't wait to ride my new bike!"

2

A Batch of Trouble

Sunday night Freddie sat at his computer, adding up the profits from the weekend's cookie sales. So far his business was a major success. He and Flossie had sold even more cookies on Sunday than they had on Saturday. By the time the weather got really nice, he would have his bike. He picked up a magazine from his bed and flipped to the page he had marked. He had already picked out the bike he wanted.

Everything was going perfectly. Freddie got up from his desk and went downstairs to get something to drink. Suddenly he remembered how a few customers had said the cookies made them thirsty. Maybe I should sell lemonade, too, Freddie thought as he walked into the kitchen. He stopped short.

"Hey!" he cried. "Cut it out!"

Flossie was hunched over a tin of cookies. She turned around slowly. "Cut what out?" she said in an innocent voice.

"I saw you eating the cookies we made to sell tomorrow afternoon," said Freddie. "How many did you have?"

"I didn't have any," Flossie protested. "I was just checking them. You know, to see if they were keeping fresh in there." She pointed to the tin.

Freddie frowned. "You have a huge smudge of chocolate on your face," he told her.

Flossie grabbed a napkin off the counter and wiped her face. "Oh, how did that get there?" she said.

"Look, Flossie, we're not going to make any money if you eat all the cookies." Freddie crossed his arms. "Maybe I should ask Teddy to help instead."

"But, Freddie, you promised!" Flossie cried.

Freddie sighed. He should have known not

to ask his sister to help him. She liked sweet things better than anyone he knew. "Okay," he said. "You can still help. But you have to swear you won't eat any more cookies."

"Okay," said Flossie. "I won't touch them." She put the lid back on the tin.

Freddie hoped she would stick to her promise. Flossie could probably eat up all of their profits in one afternoon!

"Hey, did you bring any cookies?" Tom Pantera asked when Freddie and Flossie walked into their classroom Monday morning.

"Yeah, I'll take two!" said Jennifer Weiss.

Freddie shook his head. "We're not selling them at school. But we'll have a stand set up at the park this afternoon. And we'll be selling them again next weekend," Freddie told everyone.

"Those were excellent," said Michael Grant. "I'll be there."

"Your cookies are okay," Brian Mueller said with a shrug. "But I think double fudge brownies are a lot better."

Freddie was puzzled. Brian had eaten four

cookies on Saturday, so obviously he didn't hate them. Could Brian be up to something? Freddie wondered. Brian was always bragging about how he could do everything better than everyone else. He liked to be the center of attention.

"That's why I'm going to start selling Brian's Best Brownies!" Brian announced.

"Are those the ones your mom bakes?" Tom asked.

Brian nodded. "She's going to help me make them. They're going to be huge and extra fudgy."

"They sound awesome!" Michael said. He licked his lips.

"When are you going to start selling them?" asked Tom.

Freddie glanced at Flossie. It looked as if she was thinking the same thing he was. Suddenly everyone had forgotten all about the Bobbseys' special oatmeal chocolate chip cookies!

"Next Saturday," said Brian.

"Great! We have a baseball game at the park at one o'clock," Tom said. "Be there."

"Don't worry, I will be," Brian told him.

Freddie was worried—and a little angry, too. How was he going to make any money now? Everyone would be running over to Brian's table, not his!

Freddie thought of the bike in the magazine. Thanks to Brian, he might never get it.

"And," Brian went on, "my brownies will be half price on Saturday. You know, like a grand opening sale."

Flossie tugged at Freddie's sleeve. "What are we going to do now?" she whispered.

"I don't know, but we'll have to think of something," Freddie whispered back. "Or else we'll be eating all those cookies ourselves!"

3

The Cookie War
Is On!

"And he's going to sell them at half price—a quarter each!" Freddie was telling Bert and Nan all about Brian Mueller's announcement that day at school. "He'll put us out of business."

"Maybe his brownies will taste terrible," Bert suggested.

Flossie shook her head. "They're delicious. He brought them to the bake sale, and I bought one."

"Just one?" Nan teased.

"It's simple," said Bert. "All you have to

do is sell your cookies for less than his brownies."

"We won't make enough money if we do that." Freddie frowned. "There has to be another way."

"I know!" Flossie cried. "We could give out free cookies, so people could see how good they are."

Freddie shook his head. "No way."

"I think Flossie has a good idea," Nan said. "But giving away whole cookies *would* be expensive. Why don't you give away little pieces?"

Freddie's eyes lit up. "Some of them *do* break when we're putting them on the racks to cool."

"You could go around the neighborhood and hand them out," Bert said. "Brian's not going to start selling the brownies until Saturday, right? You could get a jump on him."

A big smile spread across Freddie's face. "I have another idea," he told the others. "After I give out the samples, I can take orders for cookies. Anyone who places an order before Saturday will get a discount."

Nan laughed. "Freddie, you're going to make a great salesman someday."

"I can see it now." Bert groaned. "We're going to be baking cookies all week."

"Why don't Bert and I make some signs and post them around the neighborhood?" said Nan.

Bert nodded. "But what do we get out of all this?" he asked Freddie.

Freddie thought for a minute. "How about a dozen free cookies?" he said.

"Hey, that's no fair," Flossie complained. "You said I couldn't have any."

"That's because you're getting paid," Freddie reminded her. "Of course, if you want cookies instead—"

"No, I'll take the money," Flossie said quickly.

"Thanks, Mrs. Green," Freddie told the Bobbseys' housekeeper as he sealed a plastic container on Tuesday afternoon. "We couldn't have done it without you."

"You're welcome," answered Mrs. Green. "Good luck tonight!"

Freddie and Flossie had come home right after school to bake cookies. Since they didn't have enough broken ones this time, they had crumbled several cookies into samples.

After dinner Freddie and Flossie set out to visit their neighbors. "Make sure you get back before seven-thirty," Mrs. Bobbsey told the younger twins. "You still have homework to do."

"Okay," said Freddie.

"Why don't you two take Chief with you?" Mrs. Bobbsey asked. "He could use a good walk."

"Sure," said Freddie. He clipped a leash to the sheepdog puppy's collar. "Let's go, boy. Flossie, you take the sample bowl. I'll hold on to Chief."

Flossie slipped into her jacket, and the twins went out the door and down the street.

"I hope this works," Freddie said as he rang the first door bell.

"So do I," said Flossie. "This bowl is heavy."

Mr. Suhr opened the door. "Well, hello!" he said. "What can I do for you children?"

"How about trying one of our special oatmeal chocolate chip cookies?" Freddie asked. "They're made from our grandmother's secret recipe."

Mr. Suhr reached into the bowl and popped a sample into his mouth.

"Aren't they the best?" Flossie asked.

Mr. Suhr nodded. "If you have any that aren't broken, I'll take a dozen," he said.

"Great!" Freddie wrote down Mr. Suhr's name in the notebook he was using for Operation Bike. Maybe Brian would sell a few brownies, but he wasn't going to sell dozens!

"Where should we go next?" Flossie asked.

"Let's try the Moultons," Freddie said.

Suddenly Chief started barking.

Freddie bent down and stroked Chief's neck. "What's wrong, boy?" Chief barked even louder. Freddie looked around. "It's Mrs. Montgomery and her dog," he told Flossie.

Mrs. Montgomery lived a few blocks over from the Bobbseys. She waved to the twins.

Flossie hurried over to her. "Want to try our cookies?" she asked.

Mrs. Montgomery ate a sample cookie.

Then she smiled and ate another. "These are delicious," she said. She took another piece out of the bowl and chewed it. "How do you make them so soft?" she asked Flossie.

"You just—"

"We can't tell you," Freddie interrupted. "It's our grandmother's secret recipe." He glared at Flossie.

"A secret recipe, hmm?" Mrs. Montgomery took still another sample. She examined it, then popped it into her mouth.

Freddie was beginning to worry. If they stayed there any longer, Mrs. Montgomery would eat all the samples! "Actually, we're taking orders for cookies," he said as she grabbed another broken cookie.

Flossie moved the bowl out of Mrs. Montgomery's reach.

"How many would you like?" Freddie asked.

"I'll take three dozen," Mrs. Montgomery said.

"Great!" said Freddie, jotting the order down in his notebook. He was a little surprised, though. Mrs. Montgomery was very skinny. He couldn't imagine her eating so many cookies. "We're baking fresh ones Friday night. We'll deliver them on Saturday, if that's all right," Freddie told her.

Mrs. Montgomery stretched to reach into the bowl again. "Just one more to tide me over until then," she said with a laugh. "Goodbye!" She and her golden retriever walked away down the street.

"She must not have had dinner yet," Flossie said. "She ate about half our samples!"

"What's this? Is it Girl Scout season already?"

Freddie and Flossie turned around. A twelve-year-old had ridden up behind them on his bike. He was smirking at them. "Freddie, I didn't know you were a troop member," he sneered.

Freddie gripped his pencil tightly. If there was one person in the whole world he didn't like, it was Danny Rugg. Danny was in Bert and Nan's class at school. He was the biggest bully in Lakeport.

Danny climbed off his bike. "I just wanted to taste these stupid cookies. Your brother and

sister are making such a big deal about them."
He reached into the bowl and stuffed a couple
of samples into his mouth. "These aren't so
great," he said. "My mom's are about a
thousand times better."

"That's nice," said Flossie, turning to go.
She tugged Freddie's sleeve. "Come on, we
have a lot more houses to go to."

"What are you doing with that bowl of
broken-up, burned cookies anyway?" Danny
asked.

"They're not burned. And we're taking
orders from people," Freddie answered.

"I'll take ten," Danny said. Then he
grabbed a big handful of samples before
Flossie could stop him. "Never mind—I already have them!" He climbed back on his
bike. "You know, you'd get a lot more orders
if you didn't let people taste these things first."
Danny made a face.

"If they're so awful, how come you're
eating them?" Flossie asked.

Danny laughed. "These cookies aren't for
me. I'm going to feed the pigeons in the
park!" he said.

Freddie clenched his hand into a fist. Thanks to Danny, their sample bowl was empty. They wouldn't be able to take any more orders tonight.

"Good luck, Bobbseys!" Danny called out as he rode away. "You'll need it!"

4

Out the Window

"Next batch ready to go!" Bert announced. It was Friday night, and all the twins were busy baking.

"Did you remember to add the chocolate chips this time?" asked Freddie.

"Of course I did," said Bert. He handed the bowl of batter to Nan. She dropped spoonfuls of dough onto a cookie sheet and slid the sheet into the oven.

"Don't forget to set the timer," Nan told Flossie. She washed the dough off her hands and wiped them on a towel.

"I won't," Flossie promised. She was licking batter off a spoon.

"I'm sure glad this is the last batch," said Bert. "I don't think I can stir any more." He rubbed his arm.

"This is a lot more work than I thought it would be," Freddie complained. "I hope Brian's brownies turn out horrible."

"Well, there's no way he'll have this many brownies tomorrow," Bert said. "We must have made a hundred cookies so far!"

"Don't forget, Freddie," added Nan. "You've already sold half of these cookies to our neighbors."

"You put those into the delivery stack, right, Flossie?" asked Freddie.

"What do you mean?" Flossie replied.

Freddie wiped his forehead. It was pretty hot in the kitchen. The oven had been on for a long time. "I told you to count out the cookies for the special orders and put them in those boxes, remember?"

Flossie bit her lip. "Um . . ."

"Flossie! You have to help!" Freddie cried.

"I *have* been helping!" Flossie argued. "I went around with the samples after school three times this week."

"Hold on a second," said Nan, wrinkling her nose. "What's that smell?"

"Burning cookies!" said Bert. He grabbed a potholder and opened the oven door. Smoke billowed out, and Freddie could feel his eyes watering.

Flossie held her nose. "Peeu!" she yelled.

Bert set the cookie sheets on top of the stove as Nan opened the kitchen windows. "It won't take too long to air out," she said.

"Rats!" said Freddie. "Now we have to make another batch."

"You know, I can think of things I'd rather be doing," Bert complained.

"Me, too," said Flossie. "My favorite TV show is on."

"You were the one who was supposed to set the timer," Freddie told her. "It's your fault these got burned!"

Nan scraped the cookies off the pan into the trash can. "It's no use fighting, guys. We might as well get started on the next batch."

"How much sugar are we supposed to add?" Bert asked. "I keep forgetting." He reached toward the counter by the window for the

recipe. "Hey, Freddie, did you take the recipe?" he asked.

Freddie shook his head. "No, you had it."

"I don't have it anymore," said Bert.

"Wasn't it right here?" Nan looked at the counter and felt around the flour and sugar jars. "I don't see it anywhere."

"What?" Freddie jumped off his chair. "Are you saying we lost the recipe?"

"Don't panic," Nan told him. "We'll find it."

Flossie got up, too, and started looking all over the floor. "Maybe you mixed it into the batter," she said to Bert.

"Ha, ha," Bert replied. "I'm not *that* bad."

"This isn't funny, you guys!" Freddie said. "We can't lose the recipe."

"It has to be here somewhere," said Bert. He ran his hand along the edge of the window. "Hey, look at this!" he said.

"Did you find it?" asked Freddie. He rushed over to the window.

"No, but I think I know where it went," said Bert. He pointed to a chocolate smudge on the window sill.

"But there's a screen," Flossie said. "It couldn't have blown out the window."

"It didn't," said Bert. "Someone *took* it."

"How did they get through the screen?" asked Freddie.

"It's not down the way it should be," Nan observed. "Anybody could have gotten in."

"I'll bet they didn't know they were leaving a fingerprint!" Bert exclaimed. He ran into the living room and returned with his Rex Sleuther fingerprinting kit. Rex Sleuther was Bert's favorite comic-book detective.

Nan shook her head. "That doesn't make any sense. It's just a chocolate smudge. I probably made it when I was opening the windows."

Bert frowned. "You washed your hands before you opened the windows, remember? So the smudge couldn't be yours."

"Well, it could be yours, then," Nan argued.

"You have to admit it was pretty smoky in here," said Bert. "Someone could have reached in the window without us noticing."

"Maybe we threw it out by mistake," said Freddie hopefully. He started digging through the trash.

But after fifteen minutes of searching the entire kitchen, the recipe was still missing.

"Someone stole it for sure," Bert said. He went over to the window again. "And from the look of this smudge, I'd say the person was in a hurry."

"Who'd steal a cookie recipe?" asked Nan.

"I can think of a couple of people," said Freddie. And one of them would definitely have had chocolate on his hands: Brian Mueller! He'd probably been baking his double fudge brownies all evening! Freddie frowned. He wouldn't put it past Danny Rugg to try to wreck things, either—just for the fun of it.

"Are you sure you didn't put the recipe somewhere?" Bert asked Flossie.

"Yeah. Maybe she ate it by mistake," said Freddie.

"I did not!" his twin said.

"Don't blame Flossie," said Nan. "Maybe the recipe will turn up tomorrow morning."

"If it doesn't, I won't have to worry about selling more cookies than Brian," said Freddie. "I won't have practically any to sell at all!"

5

Too Many Cooks

"Was it three cups of flour or two?" asked Mrs. Green on Saturday morning. She shook her head. "I just can't remember."

"I made that batter so many times, I thought I'd memorized the recipe," Bert said. "I can't believe Grandma is away this week."

"Neither can I," grumbled Freddie. Early that morning he had called his grandmother to get another copy of her recipe. Then he'd remembered that she was in Florida, visiting friends.

"Can't we go over to Grandma's house and look around?" Freddie asked his mother.

"We don't have a key," Mrs. Bobbsey told him.

"We could go in through a window," Freddie suggested.

"Freddie, we are not going to break into your grandmother's house," Mr. Bobbsey said firmly. "That wouldn't be right."

"Don't worry," Mrs. Green said. "I'm pretty sure I know the recipe by heart."

Freddie, Bert, Nan, and Flossie all remembered different parts of the recipe—and different amounts, too! Finally they thought they had the right combination of ingredients. With Mrs. Green's help they baked a batch from the new recipe.

Freddie took a big bite of one of the new cookies after they had cooled. His heart sank. It didn't taste anything like his grandmother's. Would other people notice the difference?

Freddie ran outside. "Mom, Dad! Can you come here for a second?" Mr. and Mrs. Bobbsey were working in the backyard. "I need you to try out our cookies," said Freddie.

"Sure," said Mrs. Bobbsey, standing up.

"Mom and Dad are going to do a taste test," Freddie told everyone.

"I don't think—" Bert began.

"Shh," said Freddie. "Let them decide." He gave their parents each one cookie from the good batch, then he gave them one from that morning's batch.

"I hate to tell you this," said Mrs. Bobbsey, chewing. "But one tastes a lot better than the other." She frowned and held up the cookie from the new batch. "This one tastes like it's missing something."

"I'm afraid I agree," said Mr. Bobbsey.

Bert looked at Freddie. "I told you it wasn't worth it. The new ones don't taste the same."

"We'll keep trying," Nan told Freddie. "We'll get it right sooner or later."

"It better be sooner," said Freddie. "Before someone else starts making cookies from our secret recipe!" He still had all the cookies they'd made before the recipe was stolen. But when he ran out of them, he would be out of luck.

"Come on, Freddie. Let's bring the cookies

we have to the park," said Flossie. "If we get there before Brian, maybe we'll sell out."

If Brian had stolen the Bobbseys' secret recipe, he might be selling brownies *and* cookies, Freddie thought. They could catch him red-handed. "Let's get going," Freddie told his sister. "We don't have much time!"

"We'll keep putting up posters to advertise your cookies," said Nan.

"Why don't we tell the people who ordered cookies that there's been a slight delay and they'll get them soon?" said Bert. "That way you'll have more to sell at the park."

"Good idea!" said Freddie. "Thanks!"

He and Flossie filled their bags with cookie tins and headed to the park. "If Brian thinks he can get away with this, he's wrong," Freddie muttered as they hurried across the street.

"Do you really think Brian took the recipe?" asked Flossie.

"Sure. He's the one who's trying to outdo us with his dumb brownies," said Freddie.

"Yeah, but he lives blocks away," Flossie

pointed out. "How would he know we were making cookies?"

"He probably guessed. We told him we were selling them today," said Freddie.

"Maybe. Oh, no!" Flossie said suddenly. "Look!" She pointed toward the park entrance. A large crowd of kids had gathered.

Freddie got a terrible feeling in his stomach. "Come on, Flossie," he said. "We're not going to let Brian beat us so easily."

The twins hurried over to the picnic tables near the park entrance. A big banner that said, "Try Brian's Best Brownies! Half Price Today Only!" was draped over one table. Kids were crowded all around Brian. He had five plates of brownies, and they were selling quickly.

Freddie put down his cookies two tables over from Brian. "Bobbseys' homemade oatmeal chocolate chip cookies here!" he yelled. That was the way hot dogs were sold at the ballpark. Freddie figured he could sell cookies the same way.

At first it seemed as if no one had heard him. Then Flossie walked over to the group, holding a plate of cookies. A few kids finally wandered over to Freddie.

"How much?" one girl wanted to know.

"Thirty-five cents," said Flossie.

Freddie thought quickly. He hated to do it, but he really would have to make his cookies cheaper than Brian's brownies.

"Did she say thirty-five?" Freddie asked. "She meant twenty-five. For two."

"So much for the fair," Flossie mumbled.

"We won't make as much money, but at least we'll make some," Freddie whispered back.

But most of the kids just looked at the cookies and then walked away. They were already full from Brian's double fudge brownies! The twins' only customers were two polite women who said they couldn't pass up oatmeal chocolate chip cookies. By three o'clock the twins had sold only a dozen.

Brian, on the other hand, was practically out of brownies. "Looks like I'll have to take off pretty soon," he bragged to the Bobbseys. "I need to make some more for tomorrow."

He walked over to the twins' table. "Maybe

you should work on a new recipe," he told Freddie.

"There's nothing wrong with our recipe," Freddie replied.

"Yeah, we just can't find it," added Flossie.

Freddie cleared his throat. "What she means is that it's a *secret* recipe."

"I don't think anyone wants it," Brian scoffed. "Especially not after *I* start selling cookies."

Freddie was so mad he could feel his ears turning bright red. "You're going to sell cookies?" he asked.

Brian nodded. "Yep. Chocolate chip. My mom's making them right now."

So Brian *had* stolen their recipe, Freddie said to himself.

"Why don't you give us back our recipe?" Flossie demanded. "We know you took it!"

"I didn't take your stupid recipe," said Brian. He nodded toward the empty plates on his table. "I don't need it, anyway. You're lucky someone took yours. You're just wasting your time out here!"

Before the twins could say anything more, a man came up to the table. He was the same man who'd said their cookies weren't so great the week before. He was wearing the same clothes. They looked like some kind of uniform.

The man glanced around the park. "Not doing such good business today, are you?"

Freddie shrugged. "Not really, I guess."

"That's because I'm here," Brian told the man. "Everyone knows double fudge brownies are a lot better than boring old cookies."

The man raised one eyebrow. "You're selling brownies?"

"Do you want one?" Brian asked. "I've got a couple left."

The man shook his head and muttered something to himself. Then he walked away.

"What's with him?" asked Flossie.

"I don't know," said Freddie, "but he sure seems strange."

"Well, time to get going." Brian picked

up his cash box and shook it. "Not bad for one day. Just wait until I'm selling cookies, too!"

And just wait until I prove you stole our recipe, Freddie added to himself. I'm going to do it before next weekend, that's for sure!

6

Burned Again

When Freddie and Flossie got home, Nan and Bert were waiting for them. "We have some good news and some bad news," Bert said.

"We have *all* bad news," said Freddie, looking glum.

"What happened?" asked Nan.

Freddie told her about Brian's success at the park. "We sold hardly any cookies," he said.

"That's too bad," said Nan. "And those were the good ones, too."

"What's the other bad news?" asked Freddie.

"Well, we went around putting up posters for your cookies," Bert said. "Only as soon as we put them up, someone else took them down."

"Tell me you're kidding," said Freddie.

Nan shook her head. "Sorry."

"Maybe the wind blew them off," said Flossie.

Bert shook his head. "We taped them up pretty tightly. I don't think they would have come off unless someone ripped them off."

"But who?" asked Freddie. "It couldn't have been Brian. We were with him all afternoon. He probably got one of his friends to do it."

"I bet it was Danny Rugg," said Flossie, frowning. "He said we'd never make any money."

"But would Danny have come over here to steal the recipe?" asked Nan. "I doubt it."

Freddie told them that Brian was going to start selling cookies, too. "I think it's Brian for sure," he said.

"Rex Sleuther says sometimes the most

obvious suspect is the most innocent one," Bert said.

Freddie groaned. Bert was always quoting his favorite comic-book detective.

"Well, are there any other suspects you can think of?" Nan asked them. "Is there anyone else who doesn't seem happy about your cookies?"

"There's this guy who came by our table twice," Flossie told them. She described the man from the park. "He's always wearing this shirt with his name on it and white pants."

"What was his name?" asked Bert.

"I think it was Mike," said Freddie. "And he acted really weird."

"What do you mean?" Nan said.

Freddie shrugged. "He just wasn't very nice."

"Can you remember anything else about him?" Nan asked the twins.

Freddie shook his head. "What's the point? I know it's Brian."

"Wait!" Flossie cried. "Remember the first time that Mike guy bought cookies from us?

When he gave me the money, I got white stuff all over my hands. I bet it was flour."

"Are you sure it was flour?" Nan asked her.

Flossie nodded. "Yep, I'm sure."

Freddie looked at his twin doubtfully. "So what does that prove?"

"It proves," Bert said, "that *he* was doing some baking, too!"

"And if he wears a uniform, then he might work in a bakery," Nan added.

Bert went out into the hallway and grabbed the telephone book with the yellow pages. "Maybe we can figure out which one," he said.

"You guys are all wrong about this," Freddie said with a sigh.

Bert flipped to the bakery listings in the phone book. "There's Baker's Bakery, Denny's Doughnuts, and—hey, listen to this! Mike's Pastry Shop on Elm Avenue. That's right across from the park."

"If he works in a bakery, that would explain the smudge on the windowsill," said Nan. "He could have had chocolate on his hands from work. Bakers work at night, too."

"Maybe we should pay Mike a visit on Monday," Bert suggested.

"*You* can if you want, but I think it's a waste of time," said Freddie. "Why would a real baker care about me selling cookies?"

"I don't know," admitted Nan.

"Maybe Grandma's recipe is better than his," said Flossie.

Freddie pointed at the stack of full tins on the kitchen table. "I don't think so."

"That reminds me. Mr. Suhr wants you to bring his cookies over right away," said Bert.

"Okay," said Freddie. "I'll do it after dinner. What about Mrs. Montgomery? Does she want hers?"

"That's the good news. She said she's not in any hurry," Nan told him. "That means you can sell what's left of the original cookies at the park tomorrow."

"That's funny," said Flossie. "It seemed like she couldn't live without them the other day."

"Maybe she was just hungry," said Bert.

"I think she was doing some of her own baking," said Nan. "The house smelled pretty good when we were there."

Freddie sighed. Suddenly no one wanted to buy his cookies. And he was nowhere near having the money he needed for his bike.

On Sunday it rained. Freddie was almost glad he didn't have to go to the park and try to sell the cookies he had left. Besides, it gave him time to come up with a plan.

Freddie knew he had to stop Brian from selling cookies before he got started. And to do that, he had to prove that Brian was the one who had stolen his recipe.

All Sunday afternoon Freddie tried to think of a way to catch Brian. Finally an idea came to him.

Brian had stolen Freddie's recipe because he couldn't beat him fair and square. He'd probably steal *any* recipe the Bobbseys had!

All Freddie had to do was get Brian to steal another. He could catch him in the act!

Freddie didn't have any other secret recipes. But he could *pretend* he did. Freddie knew that Brian would be interested—interested enough to fall into his trap.

7

Setting the Trap

On Monday Freddie set the first part of his plan in motion. He headed over to the park after school because Brian had said he'd be there. A big group of kids from school were watching a baseball game. Freddie saw his best friend, Teddy Blake. Brian was watching, too.

Freddie went over to join the group. "Hi, guys," he said. "Who's playing?"

"Sixth grade against the seventh," Tom Pantera told him.

Freddie looked out at the field. Danny Rugg was playing third base. He watched as Danny fielded a grounder.

Freddie had already told his best friend about the plan, and Teddy had volunteered to help. Now Freddie nudged his best friend's arm.

"Hey, Freddie, when are you selling cookies again?" Teddy asked loudly.

"Next Saturday," Freddie said. "And guess what? My grandmother's giving me the recipe for her super cookie."

"Super cookie?" Brian asked. "What's that?"

"It's the best!" Freddie said. He had to make the super cookie sound really good or else Brian wouldn't be interested. "It has all kinds of candy in it, plus peanut butter, butterscotch, and chocolate."

Brian's eyes lit up. "That sounds great," he said. Then he looked around at everyone else. "But not as good as double fudge brownies."

"What's the deal with you guys, anyway?" Tom asked. "You never made things to eat before."

"I'm trying to save money for a new bike," Freddie admitted.

"And I want to buy Marxus, that new video

game," said Brian. "You know, the one with all the cages you have to get out of? My parents said I could have it if I earned the money."

Freddie looked at him in surprise. Maybe Brian wasn't just trying to be better than him. Maybe Brian wanted extra money, too.

But Freddie was going to follow through with his plan. After all, Brian had stolen his idea of selling cookies. And he had stolen Freddie's recipe, too!

"I'll have my super-duper cookies next Saturday," Freddie announced. "They're so awesome, you won't believe it when you taste them."

"If they're anything like your oatmeal ones, you'll probably be poisoned!" called Danny Rugg, walking off the field.

Freddie gritted his teeth. If Brian wasn't trying to mess things up for him, then Danny sure was.

But they wouldn't get away with it much longer!

"We went to Mike's Pastry Shop after school," Nan told Freddie when he got home.

"To check out that man who complained about your cookies."

"Was he there? What did he say?" Freddie asked.

"Did you find the recipe?" said Flossie.

"No, we didn't," said Bert. "And we're pretty sure he didn't take it—or rip down your posters."

"How could you tell?" Flossie wanted to know.

"Well, for one thing, he gave us about ten different sample cookies," Bert said. "None of them were oatmeal chocolate chip. And, no offense, Freddie, but all of them were a lot better than yours."

Freddie frowned. "What do you mean?"

"Mike's an expert," said Bert. "He can make about fifty kinds of cookies. And he has all the recipes in his head."

"Then how come he was so mad when he saw us at the park?" asked Flossie.

"He said business has been really slow lately," Nan told them. "I guess a lot of people have been buying cookies and pastries somewhere else."

"He probably wanted to check out the competition," Bert added.

"I wish!" Freddie sighed. "Well, I knew all along it was Brian."

Bert nodded. "It does look as if Brian's our prime suspect now."

"Don't forget Danny," Flossie added. "He might not want to make his own cookies, but he sure likes to make fun of ours."

"I don't think it's Danny," said Freddie. "Unless he and Brian are working together. Danny could be the one taking down the posters."

"Maybe Brian is sharing his profits with him," Nan said.

"Well, we'll know tomorrow who stole Grandma's recipe," said Freddie.

"How's that?" asked Bert.

Freddie told the others about his plan to catch Brian by pretending to have a recipe for an even better cookie. Everyone agreed the plan was a great idea.

On Tuesday afternoon Freddie and Flossie started on part two of the plan.

"Come on, Flossie," Freddie said in a loud voice when the bell rang at the end of school. "We have to put up signs on the way home."

"That's right!" Flossie practically shouted back. "We have to let everyone know about the super cookie!"

Freddie put his finger to his lips. "Don't overdo it," he whispered.

As they walked out of school, Freddie looked around to see if Brian had heard them. Brian was already climbing onto his bike. Freddie watched him pedal away.

"He's probably just doing that to make it *look* like he's going home," Freddie said.

The twins walked all around their neighborhood. They purposely passed right by Danny Rugg's house to catch his attention. Freddie taped a poster to the street lamp in front of Danny's house.

"I can't wait until we start selling these," Freddie said.

"Me, either!" added Flossie.

They were turning the corner at the end of the block when they heard a front door open and close. Freddie tried to look over his shoulder, but he didn't want to be too obvious.

The twins circled around the block. When they got back to the spot where they had placed their first poster, it was already gone!

"The plan is working so far," Freddie said. "Can you see anyone following us?"

Flossie glanced backward. "Nope," she said.

"We'll have to keep going," said Freddie.

"My legs are getting tired," Flossie complained.

Freddie rolled his eyes. "It won't take much longer," he told her.

They walked a few more blocks. All of a sudden Flossie stopped in her tracks.

"What's the matter?" Freddie asked.

"I just saw someone," Flossie whispered. "He sneaked behind that tree when we came around the corner."

Freddie's eyes lit up. "Did you see who it was?"

"No," said Flossie. "He moved too fast. He looked kind of tall."

"That's okay. I know how to get him out from behind that tree." In a loud voice

Freddie said. "We'll have to stop putting up signs now. It's time to meet Nan and Bert at Food Mart."

"Why are we meeting them there?" asked Flossie in her most innocent—and very loudest—voice.

"To get the ingredients for the super cookie. Don't you remember?" Freddie replied.

"Oh, right! I can't wait. They're going to be yummy!" Flossie exclaimed.

Freddie couldn't wait, either. The sooner they caught the recipe thief, the sooner he'd have his new bike.

"Come on, Flossie," he said. "Let's go!"

8
Seeing Double

All four Bobbsey twins met outside the supermarket. "Make sure you get a good shopping cart," Freddie told Bert. "We might have to chase him."

"It looks pretty crowded in here," Nan said when the door opened for them. "I hope we don't have to chase anyone."

Bert pushed the cart through the doors and around to the first aisle. "Let's see. Here's the first thing we need. Prunes." He grabbed a box and tossed them into the cart. "What's next?"

Freddie looked at the index card in his hand.

He had written down a list of things that would taste terrible together. "Marshmallow topping," he announced.

Nan wrinkled her nose. "I'm glad we don't really have to make these," she whispered.

Freddie grinned. The way he'd planned it, there would be only two carts in the supermarket with the same items in them. "We need nuts, too," he said.

"What kind?" asked Bert.

"I don't know. I can't make out this word." Freddie pretended to study the card. "You know Grandma's writing."

Bert leaned over to take a look. "Pistachio," he said. "What else?"

Nan and Flossie looked as if they were going to burst out laughing. "Some super cookie!" Nan giggled.

"Super *awful!*" said Flossie.

"Shh!" Bert whispered. "I'm trying to listen for footsteps behind us."

"Yeah. Keep your eyes open for Danny and Brian," Freddie told his sisters.

"I think we should head to the candy aisle," Nan said.

Freddie nodded. "I told Brian there was a ton of candy in the new cookies. I know he'll look for us there."

"I'll walk a few paces behind," said Bert. "I'll watch for any suspicious-looking people."

"You don't have to look out for anyone except Brian or Danny," Freddie reminded him.

Bert shrugged. "You never know. Rex always says to keep your eye out for the—"

Bert kept talking, but Freddie hurried ahead to catch up with Nan. Rex Sleuther could say all he wanted. Freddie had already solved *this* case!

They stopped in front of the candy, and Nan turned around. "Where's Flossie?"

"Beats me," said Freddie. "Maybe she's following Bert."

"Okay, we may as well get started," said Nan. "What kinds do we need?"

Freddie consulted his imaginary recipe again. "We need licorice, cinnamon hearts, and lime gumdrops. And don't forget the three bags of butterscotch chips."

Flossie was crouching behind a stack of green bean cans at the end of the aisle. She planned to wait there until either Brian or Danny showed up. She figured it wouldn't be too long a wait. They had to be right behind Freddie and Nan if they wanted to hear about the recipe.

Flossie felt her mouth begin to water as she watched Freddie dump all that candy into their cart.

Then she heard Nan say, "Well, I guess that's it except for these." Nan put a bag of caramels in the cart and walked off with Freddie.

Brian will be coming along any second, Flossie told herself. The only problem was, her legs were beginning to hurt from squatting. She rubbed her legs with her hands. "Just a few more minutes," she whispered.

But when Flossie looked back up over the stack of cans, she could hardly believe it. There was a cart filled with prunes, marshmallow topping, licorice, lime gumdrops, and funny pink nuts!

She stood up quickly, and her sneaker

caught one of the cans near the bottom. The can went skidding across the floor. Flossie jumped back as a few more cans toppled to the floor. Uh-oh, she thought. I hope the rest stay in place.

Suddenly the entire stack collapsed! Cans of green beans came crashing down all around Flossie. They made loud bangs as they hit the floor, and she put her hands over her ears.

Even so, she could hear a voice over the loudspeaker system saying, "Manager to aisle six, manager to aisle six." Flossie looked up at the big number 6 on the sign above her. Now she was in big trouble!

"Are you all right, little girl?" a woman holding a baby asked Flossie.

Flossie nodded and looked around. There were about a hundred cans of green beans on the floor. People were coming over to see what all the noise was. Flossie didn't see Danny or Brian anywhere.

Nan rushed to Flossie's side, leaving the Bobbseys' cart in the next aisle. "Are you okay?"

"I'm fine. *And* I found the recipe thief!" Flossie said.

Freddie grinned. "That's great! Where is he?"

But Flossie didn't get a chance to answer. A man wearing a red coat was coming toward them. The word *Manager* was sewn above his coat pocket. "What happened here, young lady?" he asked Flossie.

Flossie widened her eyes. "I was just walking by. I guess I must have bumped one of the cans."

"*One* of the cans?" The manager frowned and tapped his foot against the floor. Two stock boys began to pick up the cans and stack them neatly.

"I only touched one," Flossie said. That was true. It wasn't her fault all the cans were connected. Besides, she had to hurry and get rid of the manager so they could catch the thief.

"Well . . . okay," said the manager. "Since no one was hurt, I guess everything's all right here." But he looked at Flossie as if she were a

69

troublemaker. "Is she your sister?" he asked Nan.

Nan nodded. "I'll make sure she stays with me from now on," she promised.

"Good," said the manager. "I don't want to catch you—"

Luckily, the loudspeaker crackled again. "Manager to checkout, please," a woman's voice said.

The manager hurried off down the aisle. Flossie heaved a sigh of relief. "Nan!" she said, tugging at Nan's sleeve. "I saw a cart full of our weird candy. It's right—" Then she stopped. The cart she had seen two minutes before was gone!

9

In the Bag

"He's probably in the next aisle," said Freddie.

"He can't have gone far," agreed Nan. "Let's split up and search the store."

"Don't forget, we need evidence," Bert reminded everybody. "So find the cart, too."

Freddie took off for the nut section. He was sure he'd catch Brian trying to put the pistachios back. He must have seen Flossie and figured out they were watching for him, Freddie decided.

But he didn't find Brian by the nuts or the prunes or anywhere else. He circled back to the candy aisle. Brian would probably go back there once it had cleared out. But the only person he saw there was Flossie.

"No luck," Freddie told the others when they met at the front of the store.

"I didn't find the cart, either," said Bert.

"Whoever it was must have taken off when he saw Flossie," Freddie said. He tried not to feel angry toward his twin, but she had botched the perfect plan. Now they would never get their recipe back.

"There's something strange going on, though," said Nan. "I didn't see *our* cart, either." She glanced around the supermarket. "I left it just at the end of aisle five. An employee must have put all the stuff back already."

"Or maybe someone took our cart and all the things in it," Freddie said.

"Whoever it is will be sorry," said Flossie, giggling.

"Wait a minute," said Nan. She pointed toward the checkout line. "Isn't that Mrs. Montgomery?"

Freddie spun around. Sure enough, their

neighbor was just picking up a large bag of groceries. "So?" he asked.

"Well, she's the only person in here we know. And she knows about your cookies," said Nan. "Maybe *she's* the one who took the recipe."

Freddie shook his head. "Get real! What would she want with our recipe?"

"I don't know, but let's follow her," Nan said. "She just left the store."

"Be careful she doesn't see us," warned Bert.

"Okay, but we're wasting our time," Freddie answered.

Flossie and Freddie kept a few steps behind Nan and Bert as they followed Mrs. Montgomery down the street. "Remember how many samples she ate?" Flossie asked.

Freddie thought for a minute. Mrs. Montgomery *had* seemed a little eager about the cookies. "But she ordered so many," he said. "Why would she want the recipe, too?"

Bert overheard him. "She told me and Nan she didn't mind about not getting her cookies, remember?"

"Plus, she was baking something when we went to her house," Nan added. "That was Saturday—and the recipe was stolen Friday night!"

Freddie shook his head. He couldn't believe the thief had been anyone but Brian.

"Ssh," said Bert suddenly. They slowed down and tried to hide behind a large bush. Mrs. Montgomery had stopped and bent down to tie her shoelace.

"We have to find out if she has the phony ingredients in that bag," Bert whispered. "That's the only way we'll know if she's the thief."

"Okay, but how?" asked Freddie.

"The best way to catch a suspect is to—" Bert began.

"Surprise him," the other three said in unison. Freddie rolled his eyes. Bert had told them what Rex Sleuther had said about a hundred times.

"That's right," said Bert.

In the meantime their neighbor had started walking again.

Bert hurried after her as she turned up the

walk to her house. "Mrs. Montgomery!" he called. "Mrs. Montgomery, wait up! We have your cookies!"

When Mrs. Montgomery turned around, the look on her face was one of pure shock. "Oh, er, hello!" she called back. She took one hand out from under the bag to wave to the Bobbseys—and when she did, the bottom of the bag ripped.

Out tumbled a jar of marshmallow topping, a bag of pistachio nuts, a box of prunes—and three bags of butterscotch chips!

10

Chip Off the Old Block

Bert grinned at Freddie. "Didn't I tell you? Surprising the crook always works."

"I can't believe it," said Freddie.

Mrs. Montgomery's face was bright red. She didn't even try to hide the things that had fallen to the ground. "I guess I picked the wrong day to go shopping," she said with a nervous laugh.

Flossie put her hands on her hips. "Did you take our grandmother's secret recipe?" she asked.

Mrs. Montgomery looked a little surprised,

but she nodded. "Yes, I'm afraid I did," she admitted. "And I tore down your posters, too."

"Why?" asked Freddie. "You could have ordered all the cookies you wanted from us."

Mrs. Montgomery shook her head. "The cookies weren't for me to eat. I wanted to sell them."

"You're kidding!" said Freddie.

Mrs. Montgomery sighed. "You don't know how many times I've tried to make oatmeal chocolate chip cookies. But they never came out as good as yours. I figured all I needed was the right recipe."

"Where were you going to sell them?" asked Bert.

"You don't work for a bakery, do you?" Flossie asked. "Say, Mike's Pastry Shop?"

Mrs. Montgomery shook her head. "No. My husband sells newspapers at a store downtown. I thought that people would love to get cookies and pastries with their morning papers."

She looked down at the ground. "The only

trouble is, I'm a terrible cook! Even after I got your secret recipe, my cookies were awful." Mrs. Montgomery shook her head again. "I'm sorry. I didn't mean to put you out of business. I'll get your recipe."

When their neighbor disappeared into the house, Freddie turned to Nan. "Why didn't you tell me you thought it was her?"

"I didn't think it was her," said Nan. "Not until we saw her at Food Mart, anyway."

"I never suspected her, either," Bert said with a frown.

"I wasn't that far off," Flossie said. "She's kind of a baker."

"Yeah, a bad one!" Bert laughed.

Mrs. Montgomery came out the front door and handed the dog-eared index card to Freddie. "I'm very sorry," she said. "To make it up to you, I'd still like to buy the cookies I ordered. I'll pay you double for them, too," Mrs. Montgomery said. "In fact, make it five dozen cookies."

Freddie's eyes grew wide. "Really?"

Mrs. Montgomery smiled. "Bring them

over whenever you can. They're still the best oatmeal chocolate chip cookies I've ever tasted."

Nan picked up the jar of marshmallow topping from the ground. "What are you going to do with all this stuff?"

"Oh, I guess I'll use it eventually," Mrs. Montgomery answered. She started putting the cinnamon hearts back in the bag.

"Here's a tip from one bad cook to another," said Bert. "Don't use all those at once."

Mrs. Montgomery laughed. "Even *I* know that!"

Later that week the twins' grandmother came back from Florida. The Bobbseys invited her over for a big "Welcome Home" dinner.

As soon as they finished eating, Freddie started telling the story of the stolen recipe.

"So I was sure it was Brian," he went on, "because he said he was going to sell cookies, too. Plus he'd been making brownies Friday night, so I figured he left the chocolate smudge on the window."

"One of us must have done that," Nan said.

"Anyway, we tried to make your cookies without the recipe, but we couldn't," said Freddie.

Grandma Bobbsey burst out laughing.

"What's so funny?" Flossie asked.

Their grandmother tried to catch her breath. "You could have made the cookies without my recipe," she gasped. "It's on the back of the oatmeal box!"

Freddie stared at her. "You mean—"

"All I did was copy the recipe onto an index card for your mom's recipe box," said Grandma Bobbsey.

"But, Grandma, you told us it was a secret recipe!" said Flossie, groaning.

Grandma Bobbsey shook her head. "The only change I make in the recipe is that I don't bake them as long as it says on the box."

"Then how come everyone thought ours were so special?" asked Freddie.

"Probably because you told them they were," said Mr. Bobbsey. "You were very persuasive."

"Besides, everyone loves homemade cookies," added Mrs. Bobbsey.

"I can't believe it," said Nan. "We made a mystery out of nothing!"

"Not really," said Bert. "Someone *was* ruining Freddie's business."

"Yeah. And he did it fair and square," Flossie said.

Freddie shook his head. "I guess this means I'm stuck with my old bike."

"Not necessarily," said Mr. Bobbsey. "You've saved enough for half of the bike, haven't you?"

Freddie nodded.

"How about if we loan you the other half you need?" offered Mrs. Bobbsey. "You can do some chores around the house to pay us back. And we'll make sure that Flossie has enough money to have fun at the fair next week."

"Hooray!" Flossie cried, clapping her hands.

Freddie smiled. "Thanks, Mom and Dad!" He pictured himself riding his new bicycle around town. Then he had a horrible thought. "You're not going to make me do any cooking, are you?" he asked.

Everyone laughed. "No, Freddie. I don't think so," said Mr. Bobbsey.

"Good. I've had enough sweet stuff to last a lifetime," Freddie said.

"Me, too!" added Flossie. The whole family stared at her in surprise.

"You, give up sweets?" Bert snorted.

"Speaking of sweets, I have a fresh layer cake in the kitchen," said Mrs. Bobbsey. "But everyone seems to be sick of chocolate, so I guess we'll just skip it." She began to clear the table.

"No way!" Flossie cried. She jumped up and ran into the kitchen after her mother.

"Some things never change," said Freddie.

Mrs. Bobbsey came back, carrying the cake.

Flossie brought in the cake server. "I want an extra-big piece," she said.

"Me, too!" added Freddie.

Mr. Bobbsey served everyone, and then they all started to eat their dessert.

Grandma Bobbsey wiped her mouth with a napkin. "This is delicious," she said. "You'll have to give me the recipe."

"Oh, I couldn't possibly," said Mrs. Bobbsey. She winked at Freddie. "It's a secret!"

NANCY DREW® MYSTERY STORIES By Carolyn Keene

THE HARDY BOYS® SERIES By Franklin W. Dixon